THE GUARDIANS OF RAVENSBROOK

THE MIDNIGHT BLOODLINE

ALDARA M. ZANAMI

CONTENTS

To the dear readers,

This book is dedicated to you—the reader--who inspires me to continue telling stories of bravery, love, and darkness. Your support and passion for my words drive me to explore new worlds and challenges. Thank you for embarking on this journey with me and for believing in the power of imagination.

With gratitude and affection,

Aldara M. Zanami

1

The Return

vangeline arrived in the remote village of Ravensbrook just as the sun was setting behind the hills, plunging the landscape into an ominous gloom. The village, almost uninhabited, was shrouded in a thick mist that seemed to rise from the ground itself. The icy wind whistled through the bare trees, whose branches twisted like claws in the gloom. With each step, the cobblestone beneath her feet creaked, breaking the sepulchral silence that reigned in the place.

Evangeline had received a mysterious letter from an unknown sender, urging her to return to the home of her ancestors. The letter, written in elegant but ancient calligraphy, read: "Evangeline, the fate of our family is in your hands. The curse must be broken before it is too late. Come to Ravensbrook and discover the truth that has been hidden for generations." Although she felt an inexplicable connection to this place, the fear of the unknown was palpable.

Evangeline, 28, was an intelligent and

determined young woman, with a penetrating gaze and an inquisitive mind. She had spent most of her life in the city, away from her family's dark legacy. Following the death of her parents under mysterious circumstances when she was just a child, she was sent to live with her aunt in London. There, she became a historian, specializing in genealogy and ancient legends, perhaps as a way to better understand her own past.

The Manor Ravensbrook stood imposingly at the end of the road, like a watchful sentinel of dark secrets. Its stone walls were covered with moss, and its broken windows cast haunting shadows inside. Evangeline pushed open the heavy wooden door, which opened with a heartbreaking creak, revealing a dark and dusty hallway. The air was charged with a smell of dampness and antiquity, as if time itself had stopped within those walls.

As she explored the mansion, her thoughts drifted to her parents. She had always suspected that their death was related to the family's dark history, and now, upon returning, she was determined to uncover the truth. The mansion was in a state of advanced decay, with dust-covered furniture and spider webs hanging like funeral veils in every corner.

She climbed the creaking stairs to the second floor, where the family rooms were located. Each step resounded in the void, as if the house itself were alive and attentive to her presence. She entered the room that had been her mother's and found an old portrait hanging on the wall. It was her great-grandmother, a woman with a stern and sad look. The sight of the portrait left her frozen, but also more determined to discover the truth and end the curse.

2

The Charter

Evangeline sat down at the old desk in the study, unfolding the letter that had brought her back to Ravensbrook. The handwriting was elegant and old-fashioned, and the message was enigmatic. "Evangeline," she began, "the fate of our family is in your hands. The curse must be broken before it is too late. Come to

Ravensbrook and discover the truth that has been hidden for generations."

Reading the letter left her with more questions than answers. Determined to find clues, she made her way to the local library, an equally ancient structure that stood in the center of town like a monument to forgotten times. The shelves were filled with dusty books and aged manuscripts, and the atmosphere was permeated with a reverential silence.

In the library, she met the town historian, Mr. Grayson. He was an older man with a worn appearance, but his eyes shone with a lively intelligence and a spark of curiosity. Mr. Grayson, a former history teacher, had lost his family to the curse that plagued

Ravensbrook. He agreed to help Evangeline in her quest, moved by the desire to find peace for his own soul and put an end to the tragedy that had tormented the people for centuries.

Mr. Grayson began to tell her the history of the town and his family, a history full of shadows and secrets. He told her of how Evangeline's family had once been powerful and respected, but that a series of tragic events had led to their decline and isolation. With each word, the mystery deepened, and Evangeline felt like she was beginning to unravel a web of deception and darkness that had remained hidden for far too long.

Throughout their conversation, Evangeline also shared details of her life with Mr. Grayson. She told him about her childhood in London, her studies in history and genealogy, and her determination to discover the truth about her parents' deaths. Grayson, moved by her story, promised her that he would do everything he could to help her in her search.

3

The Mansion

Evangeline and Mr. Grayson walked together to Ravensbrook Manor. On arrival, they were greeted by the housekeeper, Mrs. Wilkes, a middle-aged woman with a stern but kind look. She had served the family for decades and knew every corner of the mansion. Mrs. Wilkes had the countenance of someone who had seen too much, her dark eyes reflecting a mixture of sadness and resignation.

As Mrs. Wilkes showed them around the mansion, she talked about her own son, who had been a victim of the curse. It was evident that her loyalty to Evangeline's family was deeply rooted, fueled by personal tragedy and a sense of duty that kept her tied to the place. She told them how her son had mysteriously disappeared one night and how his body had been found days later, lifeless, on the grounds of the mansion. The loss had devastated her, but it had also motivated her to stay and protect the mansion in honor of her memory.

While exploring the mansion, Evangeline found another ancient portrait of a woman who looked a lot like her. She was her great-grandmother, the first victim of the curse. The sight of the portrait left her frozen, but also even more determined to discover the truth and end the curse. Mrs. Wilkes made way to her great-grandmother's bedroom, a place that seemed frozen in time—antique furniture, lace curtains, and intact personal belongings created an unsettling atmosphere, as if her great-grandmother's presence still lingered there.

In their search, they also found the old garden of the mansion, now covered with weeds and vines. Mrs. Wilkes recalled how the garden used to be the pride of the family, filled with exotic flowers and rare plants. It was a place where Evangeline's great-grandmother spent hours, growing and caring for the plants with dedication. This detail gave Evangeline an insight into her ancestor's daily life and the deep connection she had to the mansion.

4

The Curse Revealed

Mr. Grayson took Evangeline to his office, where he showed her old documents and history books detailing the curse. The story was horrifying: centuries ago, an ancestor of Evangeline's had made a pact with a vampire, Lord Thorne, to save the town from famine. In return, every hundred years, a family member had to be sacrificed to keep the peace.

With each generation, the spirits of the sacrificed remained in the mansion, unable to find rest. Lord Thorne, the vampire who had initiated the curse, was still lurking in the shadows, waiting for the moment to claim his next victim. Mr. Grayson showed her ancient manuscripts describing dark rituals and pacts sealed with blood, and the magnitude of the danger became clearer to Evangeline.

The documents also contained accounts of past sacrifices, detailing how each victim had met their tragic fate. Some had been taken away in the middle of the night, others had disappeared without a trace, and all had left a trail of pain and suffering. The realization of this dark history weighed on Evangeline, but it also fueled her determination to find a way to break the curse and free her family from the endless cycle of death and despair.

Evangeline also found a letter from her great-great-grandfather, written to his wife shortly before he was sacrificed. In the letter, he spoke of the fear and despair he felt, but also of the hope that one day someone in his family would find a way to free them from the curse. These words resonated in Evangeline's heart, giving her the strength to continue her search.

5

The First Apparition

Evangeline experienced her first encounter with a malevolent spirit in the mansion. She was alone in her room when she felt an intense cold that seemed to emanate from the walls themselves. The room was filled with an ethereal mist and she saw a spectral figure approaching her with a look of despair. It was his great-grandmother, whose eyes reflected infinite sadness and a silent warning.

The encounter left her terrified, but it also provided a clue to her family's fate. The great-grandmother had been the first to suffer the curse, and her spirit was trapped in the mansion, desperately seeking to free her offspring. Evangeline attempted to communicate with her, but the apparition faded before she could get clear answers.

Terrified but determined, Evangeline decided to investigate more about her great-grandmother. She found a journal hidden in a secret dresser drawer, filled with entries detailing his life before and after the curse. The words written on those pages were a testament to her great-grandmother's suffering and struggle, and offered clues as to how she could break the curse that had fallen on her family.

The diary revealed the early days of the curse, the fear that spread through the family, and the desperate measures that were taken to protect the children. She also described her great-grandmother's relationship with her husband, a brave man who tried to stand up to Lord Thorne and who ended up being one of the first victims. These entries offered an intimate glimpse into her great-grandmother's life and the horror she had experienced.

6

The Elders of the People

Evangeline and Mr. Grayson decided to visit the village elders, who had knowledge of the curse. The first stop was at the home of Miss Haversham, a recluse who lived in a house full of dark ritual books and dried herbs hanging from the ceiling. Miss Haversham had a piercing gaze and an aura of mystery that made

Evangeline uncomfortable.

Miss Haversham revealed that her family had been involved in the rituals that kept the curse active, and that she herself had witnessed some of those rituals in her youth. She told her how Evangeline's ancestors had sealed the pact with Lord Thorne and the sacrifices that had been made to maintain it. As she spoke, Evangeline felt like she was listening to a story straight out of a nightmare, but she knew that every detail was crucial to understanding and breaking the curse.

Then, they visited Father Benedict, the village priest who had tried to protect the inhabitants from evil forces for years. Father Benedict was a man of deep faith, with a calm voice and a reassuring presence. He told them stories of failed exorcisms and restless spirits that had plagued the village for generations. His knowledge of religious rituals and his commitment to protecting the people made him a valuable ally to Evangeline in her fight against darkness.

During these visits, Evangeline also met other key characters in the town. There was Clara, Miss Haversham's brave young granddaughter, who had learned about dark rituals from her grandmother and was willing to help Evangeline. She also met Jonathan, the son of the village blacksmith, who had lost his younger brother to the curse and was now seeking revenge against the dark forces that lurked in Ravensbrook.

7

Forbidden Love

While investigating, Evangeline discovered the story of a forbidden love between her ancestor, Amelia, and a vampire hunter named Marcus. Amelia had been a young noblewoman, destined to marry a man of her status, but her heart had been captured by Marcus, a brave outsider determined to eradicate the vampire plague from the region.

Their secret encounters and fight against the darkness ended in tragedy, with Marcus being betrayed and killed by Lord Thorne. The flashbacks showed the moments of passion and despair between them, and how their love had been a fleeting hope in the midst of darkness. Evangeline felt connected to this story, feeling that Marcus' sacrifice should be honored and his mission completed.

Amelia's diary, found in the same chamber of secrets, revealed intimate details of their relationship and Marcus' plans to destroy Lord Thorne. Through the pages, Evangeline discovered that Amelia had tried to protect Marcus until the last moment, but that their love had been destroyed by the cruelty and power of the vampire. This story of love and sacrifice resonated deeply with her, fueling her determination to finish what Marcus and Amelia had started.

In addition to details about their relationship, Amelia's diary contained descriptions of Marcus' failed attempts to destroy Lord Thorne and the obstacles they faced. Evangeline also found love letters between Amelia and Marcus, filled with hope and despair, that gave her a clearer view of the magnitude of the sacrifice they had both made.

8

The Chamber of Secrets

Evangeline discovered a secret chamber in the mansion, hidden behind a fake library. The chamber was filled with ancient texts and artifacts related to the curse. He found a journal belonging to his ancestor, detailing the pact with Lord Thorne and possible ways to break the curse. The chamber contained objects of great power, and Evangeline felt that she was one step closer to the truth.

Among the objects were protective amulets, spell books, and ancient manuscripts that described dark rituals. One of the manuscripts detailed a specific ritual that could break the curse, but required significant sacrifice. The realization of this dark history weighed on Evangeline, but it also fueled her determination to find a way to break the curse and free her family from the endless cycle of death and despair.

While examining the artifacts, Evangeline came across a series of letters between Amelia and Marcus, detailing their plans to destroy Lord Thorne and free the family from the curse. These letters revealed important details about the vampire's weaknesses and the tactics they had planned to use. With each discovery, Evangeline felt she was getting closer to the truth, but she also knew that the danger increased with each step she took toward unraveling her family's dark past.

Also in the chamber of secrets, Evangeline found an ancient map of the mansion grounds, which showed hidden areas and secret passageways. This map suggested the existence of an underground crypt, a place that could hold more answers about the curse and the victims it had claimed over the years. She decided that her next step would be to explore that crypt, hoping to find the knowledge and tools necessary to confront Lord Thorne and break the curse once and for all.

9

The Hidden Crypt

Evangeline decided to explore the hidden crypt, following the ancient map she had found in the Chamber of Secrets. With the help of Mr. Grayson and Clara, she prepared for the dangerous expedition. Clara brought with her a flashlight and some protective amulets, while Grayson carried a book of ancient spells and a ceremonial knife.

The entrance to the crypt was hidden behind a statue in the garden, covered with weeds and vines. With effort, they managed to move the statue, revealing a stone door with Latin inscriptions. Clara, who had studied the ancient languages with her grandmother, translated the inscriptions:

"Here rest the secrets of the damned. Only the pure of heart can enter."

The door opened with an ominous creak, revealing a staircase descending into the darkness. The air was heavy and humid, and the silence was almost palpable. With each step down, the feeling of being watched became more intense.

When they reached the bottom, they found themselves in a vast underground chamber, dimly lit by flaming torches in the walls. Shadows danced on the walls, creating haunting shapes. In the center of the crypt was a stone altar, surrounded by ancient sarcophagi.

Evangeline approached the altar, where she found an ancient spellbook and a series of scrolls. As she examined them, a spectral figure appeared before them. It was the spirit of Marcus, the vampire hunter. His presence filled the chamber with a mixture of sadness and determination.

"You must complete what we started," Marcus said in a voice echoing through the crypt. "Lord Thorne must be destroyed and the curse broken. Only then can our souls rest."

Evangeline felt a surge of emotions as

she heard Marcus' words. She knew that his fate was tied to that of her family and that she must find the strength to face Lord Thorne. With the help of Clara and Grayson, they began to decipher the scrolls and prepare the ritual they needed to break the curse.

10

The Preparation

ack at the Ravensbrook Manor, Evangeline, Grayson and Clara set about preparing the ritual. The scrolls detailed a complex and dangerous process that required several elements: the blood of a direct descendant, a protective amulet, and the recitation of an ancient spell at the place where the curse had originally been sealed.

While preparing the necessary elements, they found new allies. Thomas, a young blacksmith from the village who had lost his father to the curse, offered his help and knowledge of making weapons and amulets. Margaret, an elderly healer, provided herbs and protective potions, as well as her wisdom about the ancient traditions of the village.

Evangeline also took advantage of this time to get to know Clara and Grayson better. Clara told her about her childhood, growing up with her grandmother and learning about the dark rituals that had plagued her family. Grayson, for his part, shared stories of his youth, his career as a history teacher, and the tragedy of losing his wife and children to the curse.

As the day of the ritual approached, the tension increased. Evangeline couldn't help but feel overwhelmed by the magnitude of the task ahead, but the support of her new friends gave her the strength she needed to keep going. Together, they planned every detail of the ritual, aware that any mistake could prove fatal.

11

The Traitor

The night before the ritual, Evangeline had a disturbing nightmare. She dreamed of Lord Thorne, who taunted her as her loved ones fell one by one. She quickly woke up, sensing an evil presence in the mansion. She decided to patrol the house, making sure everything was in order.

When she arrived at the library, she found Jonathan, the blacksmith's son, sniffing through the old books. When confronted, he attempted to escape, but was caught by Thomas and Grayson. Under interrogation, Jonathan confessed that he had been working for Lord Thorne, handing over information in exchange for the promise that his life would be spared.

Jonathan's betrayal was a devastating blow to the group. They knew that Lord Thorne was now aware of their plans and that he could attack at any moment. They decided to rush the preparations for the ritual, aware that they no longer had the element of surprise on their side.

Jonathan, repentant, offered his help to atone for his actions. Although doubtful, they decided to give it a try under strict surveillance. With his knowledge of the vampire's defenses, Jonathan provided valuable insight into Lord Thorne's weaknesses and the traps they might encounter in his lair.

12

The Battle Begins

On the night of the ritual, the group went to the crypt where it had all begun. The atmosphere was tense and charged with energy. Evangeline, armed with the protective amulet and blood of her bloodline, led the way. Clara carried the sacred texts and protective herbs with her, while Grayson and Thomas were prepared to defend them from any attack.

When they reached the crypt, they began to prepare the altar and light the torches. Evangeline stood in the center, while Clara recited the words of the spell. Suddenly, a dark figure appeared at the entrance of the crypt. It was Lord Thorne, accompanied by a group of vengeful spirits.

The battle began with a burst of dark and light energy. The spirits attacked ferociously, but Thomas and Grayson, armed with protective amulets and ceremonial knives, repelled them. Evangeline focused on the ritual, reciting the words with determination as she felt Lord Thorne's oppressive presence approaching.

Jonathan, demonstrating his repentance, fought valiantly against the spirits, protecting Evangeline and the others. The fighting was intense and desperate, with each member of the group using all of their skills and knowledge to survive. As the ritual progressed, the crypt vibrated with increasing energy, indicating that the spell was working.

13

The Sacrifice

Evangeline felt that the ritual was reaching its climax. The words of the spell echoed in the crypt, and a bright light emanated from the altar. But then, a gloomy voice filled the air. Lord Thorne had approached, and his dark presence threatened to stop the ritual.

"Do you think you can defeat me?"

sneered Lord Thorne. "Your blood is not enough to break the curse."

Evangeline knew she had to make a significant sacrifice. With tears in her eyes, she looked at her friends and realized that she had to offer something more valuable than their blood. She decided to sacrifice her own life to break the curse and free her family.

"For my family," Evangeline whispered, as she raised the ceremonial knife over her heart.

Before she could carry out the act, Clara intervened, holding her hand. "No, Evangeline. We'll find another way."

But Evangeline was determined. "It is the only way," she said firmly. "My sacrifice will break the curse and set everyone free."

With one last glance at her friends, Evangeline recited the final words of the spell and prepared for the sacrifice. But at the last moment, Marcus, the spirit of the vampire hunter, appeared and placed his hand on Evangeline's.

"Your bravery is enough," Marcus said. "I will make the sacrifice."

With those words, Marcus took the ceremonial knife and sacrificed himself in Evangeline's place. The light in the crypt intensified, and a heart-rending scream echoed through the air as Lord Thorne disappeared into a cloud of darkness.

14

The Final Showdown

With Marcus' sacrifice, the power of the curse began to fade. However, Lord Thorne was not about to leave without a fight. Its spectral form materialized once again, weaker but still dangerous. The final confrontation between Evangeline and Lord Thorne was about to begin.

Evangeline, strengthened by Marcus'

sacrifice and determination to free her family, faced Lord Thorne with new energy, using the protective amulet she channeled the power of the ritual and directed it towards the vampire. The spirits of her ancestors appeared around her, offering their support and power.

The fighting was intense and desperate. Lord Thorne launched ferocious attacks, but Evangeline, with the help of her friends and spirits, repelled every onslaught. With each blow, she felt Lord Thorne's dark energy weakening, as the light of the ritual grew stronger.

Finally, with one last effort, Evangeline uttered the final words of the spell, channeling all of her energy into Lord Thorne. Light enveloped the vampire, and with a final scream, his form faded

into nothingness, leaving only a shadow
on the crypt floor.

51

15

The Liberation

With Lord Thorne's disappearance, the dark energy in the crypt began to dissipate. The spirits of Evangeline's ancestors, now free from the curse, began to fade, offering their blessings to Evangeline and her friends before leaving. The light emanating from the altar illuminated the crypt in an almost heavenly way, contrasting with the shadows that had dominated the place for centuries.

Evangeline, exhausted but triumphant, collapsed on the ground. Her friends surrounded her, offering words of comfort and thanks. They knew that Marcus' sacrifice and Evangeline's bravery had broken the curse and freed the family and people of Ravensbrook. Clara, with tears in her eyes, held Evangeline's hand, acknowledging the enormous sacrifice she had been willing to make.

As they exited the crypt, the atmosphere seemed to change. The air was getting lighter, and the oppressive atmosphere that had reigned for so long was slowly dissipating. The villagers, upon learning of Lord Thorne's disappearance and the breaking of the curse, gathered around Ravensbrook Manor to celebrate his release. For the first time in generations, the town of Ravensbrook was free from the shadow of darkness.

The group was received as heroes. Mrs. Wilkes, moved by the bravery of Evangeline and her friends, prepared a large meal to celebrate the liberation of the village. Villagers shared stories of hope and renewal, and joy filled the air. Yet, despite the celebration, Evangeline couldn't help but feel a lingering uneasiness. She knew that although Lord Thorne's curse had been broken, other threats still lurked in the shadows.

As the night wore on, Evangeline and her friends retreated to the mansion.

Despite her tiredness, Evangeline couldn't sleep. She got up and walked through the halls of the mansion, reflecting on everything that had happened. In the library, she found Grayson going through old manuscripts, looking for any clues of future threats.

"You know this isn't over, do you?" said Evangeline, breaking the silence.

Grayson nodded solemnly. "Darkness always finds a way back. We must be prepared for whatever comes."

16

The Reconstruction

With the curse broken and the threat of Lord Thorne removed, the people of Ravensbrook began a process of rebuilding. Evangeline, along with her new friends Clara, Grayson, Thomas and Jonathan, set about restoring Ravensbrook Manor and revitalising the village. The villagers, inspired by his bravery, came together in a collective effort to bring Ravensbrook back to life.

Evangeline became a respected leader in the community, using her knowledge of history and genealogy to help villagers discover their own family legacies and connections. Clara and Grayson, with their expertise in ancient rituals and knowledge, helped establish new traditions and ceremonies that honored the past without repeating the mistakes of yesteryear.

While rebuilding the mansion, they found more secret chambers and hidden passageways. In one of the chambers, they discovered a chest filled with ancient artifacts, including spell books and protective amulets. These discoveries provided a valuable source of knowledge and power, which they used to protect the village from future threats.

Thomas, the young blacksmith, dedicated himself to teaching the young people of the village the skills of his trade, while Margaret, the elderly healer, continued to provide her knowledge and remedies to those in need. Jonathan, having demonstrated his repentance and bravery, became a valued member of the community, working tirelessly to protect Ravensbrook from any future threats.

During this time, Evangeline also discovered more about her own family and their connection to the mansion. She found ancient diaries and letters that revealed the history of her ancestors and their struggles against darkness. These documents gave her a new perspective on her legacy and the importance of protecting Ravensbrook.

17

A New Beginning

As time went on, Ravensbrook flourished under the leadership of Evangeline and her friends. The houses were restored, the fields were cultivated again and life returned to the streets of the village. The shadow of the curse faded, replaced by a new era of hope and prosperity.

Evangeline found in Ravensbrook a true

home, a place where she could honor the memory of her parents and ancestors, while building a better future for generations to come. Her relationship with Clara and the others grew stronger, creating an unbreakable bond that brought them together as a new family.

During a meeting in the town square, Evangeline announced the formation of a community council, where all villagers would have a say in important decisions. This council included representatives from each family, ensuring that everyone's needs and concerns were heard and addressed.

Clara and Grayson, with their knowledge of ancient traditions, helped establish new festivities and rituals that celebrated Ravensbrook's history and culture. These celebrations not only honored the past, but also strengthened the sense of community and unity among the villagers.

One day, while exploring the nearby forests, Evangeline found an ancient temple in ruins. She decided to restore it and turn it into a place of learning and reflection, where villagers could study ancient history and arts. This temple became a symbol of the new era of Ravensbrook, bridging the past with the present.

18

The Eternal Guard

Despite the peace that now reigned in Ravensbrook, Evangeline knew that there would always be threats hidden in the shadows. She decided to form a special guard, composed of the bravest and most loyal members of the village, to protect Ravensbrook from any evil that might arise in the future.

The guard, called "The Eternal Guard," included Clara, Grayson, Thomas, Jonathan, and other villagers dedicated to protecting the town. Together, they patrolled the boundaries of Ravensbrook, watching for any signs of danger and keeping alive the memory of the sacrifices they had made to secure peace.

During their patrols, they discovered indications of dark activities in the vicinity of the village. They found strange symbols etched into trees and rocks, and traces of dark rituals performed in secret. These discoveries reminded them that the fight against darkness would never really end.

Evangeline and the Eternal Guard met regularly to discuss their findings and strategize how to deal with any potential threats. They used the knowledge and artifacts they had discovered in the mansion to strengthen the town's defenses and protect its inhabitants.

One day, during a night patrol, Clara and Grayson encountered a group of outsiders performing a dark ritual in the woods. They confronted the intruders, discovering that they were members of an ancient cult that worshipped a being even more powerful than Lord Thorne. Although they managed to stop the ritual, they knew that this was just the beginning of a new threat.

19

The Ravensbrook Legacy

Over time, Evangeline decided to write the story of her family and the fight against Lord Thorne, so that the sacrifice and bravery of those who had fought the darkness would never be forgotten. Her book, titled "The Ravensbrooks' Legacy," became a seminal work in the town's library, a constant reminder that courage and determination can overcome any curse.

The book also served as a guide for future generations, teaching them about the importance of unity, family, and fighting injustice. Evangeline hoped her story would inspire others to face their own challenges with the same courage and determination.

While writing, Evangeline was also reflecting on her own life and her role in Ravensbrook's story. She remembered the moments of doubt and fear, but also those of hope and triumph. She knew that while darkness would always find a way back, Ravensbrook's spirit was strong and resilient.

The book was published and distributed

to the villagers, who read it with reverence and pride. She became a source of inspiration and strength, uniting the community in their commitment to protecting Ravensbrook from any future threats.

Eventually, Evangeline retired from her daily duties, trusting that Clara, Grayson, and the others would continue their work. She spent her days in the restored temple, teaching the town's youth about Ravensbrook's history and traditions.

Epilogue

espite the efforts of the Eternal Guard, the sense of unease persisted in Ravensbrook. Clara, now leader of the Guard, looked out of the window of the Manor Ravensbrook into the forest surrounding the village. She felt a disturbance in the air, an unsettling sensation that she hadn't felt in years. She knew that although Lord Thorne's curse had been broken, other threats still lurked in the darkness.

One day, while exploring the ancient texts in the chamber of secrets, Clara found a manuscript she had never seen before. Its pages were filled with symbols and warnings about an evil even older than Lord Thorne. As she read the words, a shiver ran down his spine.

She knew that a new danger was coming, and that the fight to protect Ravensbrook was not over. Determined, Clara summoned the members of the Eternal Guard and showed them the manuscript. Together, they vowed to confront any threat that would attempt to destroy the peace they had achieved.

As Clara closed the manuscript, a shadow moved in the corner of the chamber. She whispered promises of vengeance and chaos, suggesting that the real battle had only just begun.

"The Rise of the Shadow"

Get ready for the thrilling continuation of the saga with "Rise of the Shadow." In this new installment, Clara and the Eternal Guard will face an evil even older and more powerful than Lord Thorne. Peace in Ravensbrook is once again at stake, and the fate of the town will depend on the bravery and determination of its heroes to confront the new darkness that lies ahead. Don't miss this epic battle between light and shadow!

About the Author

Aldara M. Zanami

Aldara M. Zanami is an author known for her ability to weave stories that combine the supernatural with the human in deeply resonant ways. With a passion for mystery, the paranormal and emotionally intense narrative, Aldara has conquered the hearts of readers around the world.

Born in a small village steeped in legends, Aldara grew up surrounded by ancient stories and whispers of the unspeakable. From an early age, she found solace and adventure in the pages of books, developing a deep love for literature that led her to pursue writing. Her fascination with vampires, ghosts, and family curses is reflected in her work, where each story is an exploration of darkness and redemption.

Aldara is not only an accomplished storyteller, but also a passionate advocate for marginalized voices and untold stories. With each book, she seeks to bring complex characters and worlds rich in detail to life, offering her readers a literary experience that goes beyond the ordinary.

In his spare time, Aldara enjoys the tranquility of nature, where he finds inspiration for her novels. She lives in an old house with her husband, two mischievous cats, and an impressive collection of antique books and mystical objects. Every corner of her home reflects her love of the arcane and the mysterious, fueling her creativity and her desire to continue exploring the boundaries of fantasy narrative.

"The Midnight Blood" is a testament to hwe talent and dedication to the craft of storytelling. Through this work, Aldara invites readers to join her on an unforgettable journey through the dark corridors of Ravensbrook, where bravery and determination face the forces of evil.

.